D0546215

Mr Krispell
BOOKS
Brimming with imagination!
This Book Belongs To

For
Ollie, Rosie and Anastasia
Nehemiah 8:10
The Joy of the Lord is my strength.
Menu

Mr Krispell's Kids JOKE BOOK

Hundreds of Jokes and silly Poems!

written and illustrated By Mr Krispell

First Edition

While searching for the Emu
My sister got lost at the zoo
She got into a rage
And was put in a cage
I visit when I've nout to do

How do you know
if a snake has sent you
a valentines card?
It's sealed with
a hiss.

What's the best way
to brush your hare?
Hold its long ears firmly,
whilst brushing gently.

What do Cats
call mice?
Delicious!

How do you save
a drowning mouse?
Give it Mouse-to-Mouse
resuscitation!

Why shouldn't you
listen to a farmer, when
he's milking his cows?
He talks Udder Nonsense!

What's smelly and
jumps all over Australia?
A Kanga-Poo!

Why did the Poodle
marry the Golden Retriever?
She found him very fetching.

Where do dogs park their cars?
In the Barking Lot!

Why couldn't Noah catch many fish?
He only had two worms!

Where do young cows go to lunch?
The Calf-eteria.

Where can you find old cow bones?
In the Moo-seum

Where do sheep go after high school?
Ewe-niversity!

What did the farmer do when his pig had a heart attack?
He called the Ham-bulance!

Hambulance

What goes trot-dash-trot-dash-dash-dash?
Horse code.

What do you call
a big cat who lives by
a pond?
A Duck-filled-fatty-puss.

First cat; Where do
fleas go in winter?
Second cat; Search me.

What is Elsa the
elephant's middle name?
The.

What has large antlers,
Has a very high voice
and wears white gloves?
Mickey Moose.

What instrument squeaks
when you blow into it?
A Mouse organ.

What pet makes the
loudest noise?
A Trumpet!

Sign in shop window:
For Sale, pedigree Doberman.
House trained. Eats anything.
Very fond of children!

What's worse than raining cats and dogs?
Hailing taxi cabs!
Where do ants go to eat, after a hard days work?
To a Restaur-ant.
What dog won't stop crying?
A Chi-Wa-Wa.
How do cats keep their soda cold?
Mice cubes.
Where do frogs keep their jackets?
In the Croak room.
What fish do you meet in hospital?
Sturgeons!
How do you communicate with a deaf pig?
Use Swine language!

What's as big as a Hippo
yet weighs zero pounds?
A Hippo's shadow.

How did the farmer
know that the fox stole
his chicken?
The pig squealed on him.

How do you stop an
elephant from smelling?
Tie a knot in his trunk.

What do you give
a sick pig?
Oinkment.

What was the tortoise
doing on the highway?
About ten yards an hour.

What do you give
a sick lemon?
Lemonade.

What's grey has four legs and
a trunk?
A mouse going on vacation.

What do you call someone who cuts the sea bed?
A prawn-mower

How do cats celebrate when they move into a new home?
With a Mouse-warming party.

"Excuse me, do you have any dogs going cheap?"
"No sir, ours just go Woof Woof."

What do you get if you cross a sheepdog with a bunch of tulips?
Collie-flowers.

What do you call a pony with a cough?
A little horse!

What bird sits in a field with binoculars?
A Stare-crow.

How does a chicken tell the time?
One O' Cluck, two O' Cluck, Three O' Cluck

What kind of language
do hedgehogs speak?
Spine language.
What do you get
if you cross a dog with
an omelet?
Pooched eggs.
What did the mouse
say when he broke
his teeth?
Hard cheese!
What type of shoes
do bears wear?
None, they go bear foot.
Why do cows lie
down in the cold?
To keep each
udder warm.
What do you get if
you pour hot water down
a rabbit hole?
Hot cross bunnies!
How do chickens communicate with each other?
By Walkie-turkey!

Knock, Knock
Knock knock!
Who's there?
Doris.
Doris who?
Doris closed, that's
why I'm knocking!
Knock, knock!
Who's there?
Eve
Eve who?
Eve ho me
hearties!
Knock, knock!
Who's there?
Howard
Howard who?
Howard I know?
Knock, knock!
Who's there?
Aunt.
Aunt who?
Aunt these jokes
terrible!
Knock, knock!
Who's there?
Harry.
Harry who?
Harry up and
open the door!
Knock knock!
Who's there
Abbot.
Abbot who?
Abbot time you
let me in!
Knock, knock.
Who's there?
Water.
Water who?
Water you doing
in my house?
Knock, knock
Who's there?
Pooch.
Pooch who?
Pooch your arms
around me!
Knock, knock
Who's there?
P.
P who?
Well, thanks for
telling me I smell?

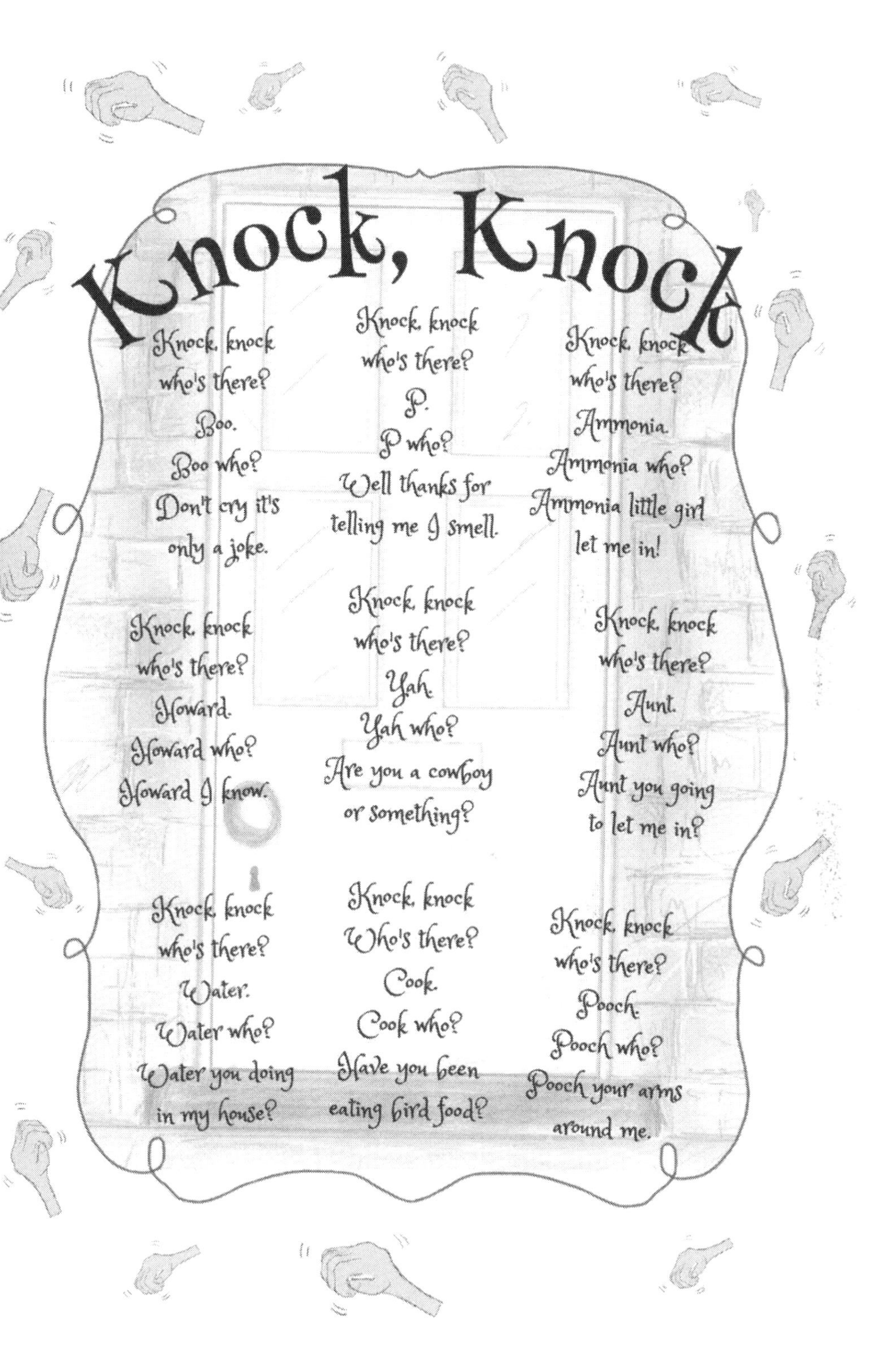
Knock, Knock
Knock, knock
who's there?
Boo.
Boo who?
Don't cry it's
only a joke.
Knock, knock
who's there?
P.
P who?
Well thanks for
telling me I smell.
Knock, knock
who's there?
Ammonia.
Ammonia who?
Ammonia little girl
let me in!
Knock, knock
who's there?
Howard.
Howard who?
Howard I know.
Knock, knock
who's there?
Yah.
Yah who?
Are you a cowboy
or something?
Knock, knock
who's there?
Aunt.
Aunt who?
Aunt you going
to let me in?
Knock, knock
who's there?
Water.
Water who?
Water you doing
in my house?
Knock, knock
Who's there?
Cook.
Cook who?
Have you been
eating bird food?
Knock, knock
who's there?
Pooch.
Pooch who?
Pooch your arms
around me.

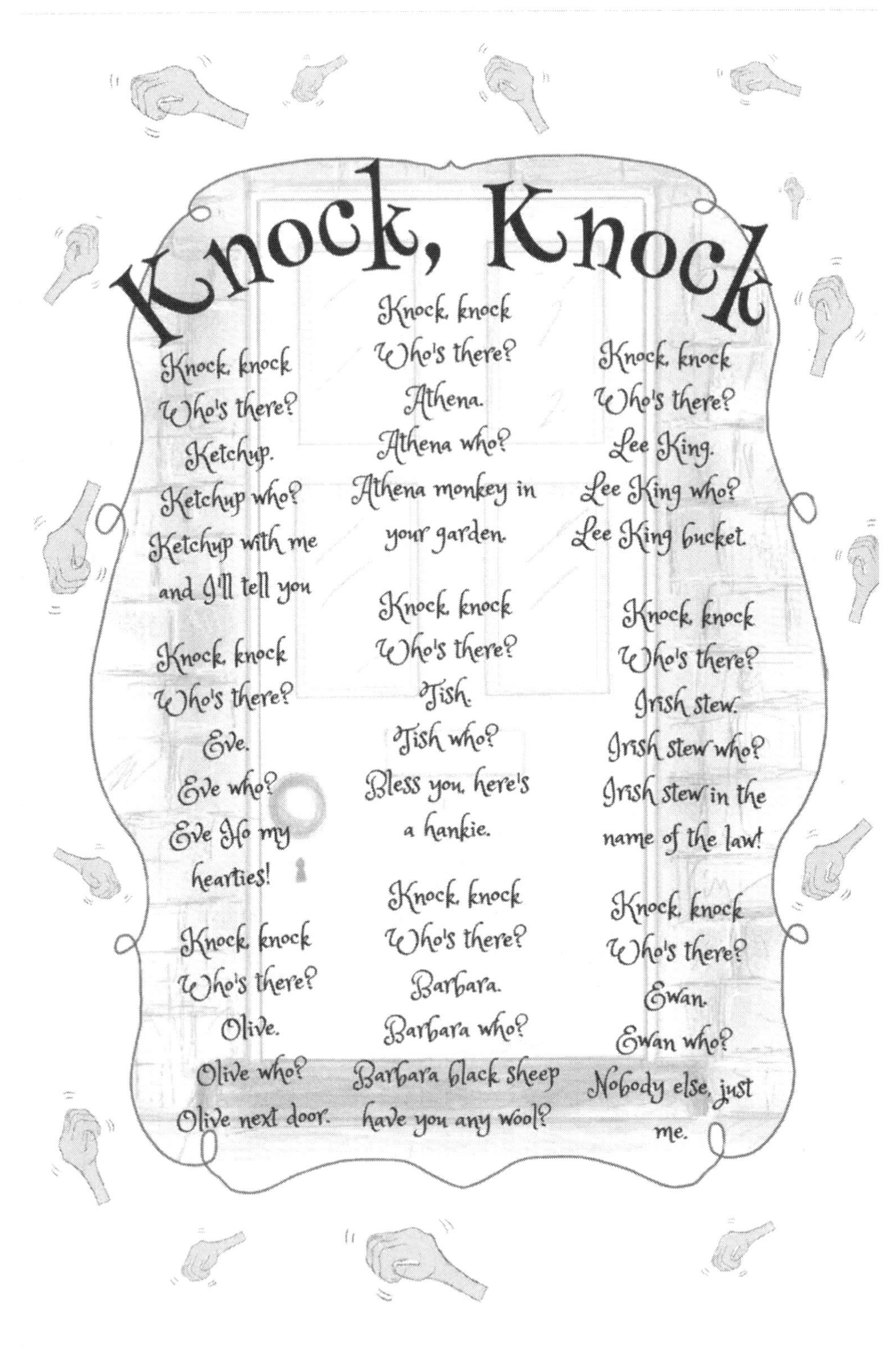
Knock, Knock
Knock, knock
Who's there?
Ketchup.
Ketchup who?
Ketchup with me and I'll tell you
Knock, knock
Who's there?
Eve.
Eve who?
Eve Ho my hearties!
Knock knock
Who's there?
Olive.
Olive who?
Olive next door.
Knock, knock
Who's there?
Athena.
Athena who?
Athena monkey in your garden.
Knock, knock
Who's there?
Tish.
Tish who?
Bless you, here's a hankie.
Knock, knock
Who's there?
Barbara.
Barbara who?
Barbara black sheep have you any wool?
Knock, knock
Who's there?
Lee King.
Lee King who?
Lee King bucket.
Knock, knock
Who's there?
Irish stew.
Irish stew who?
Irish stew in the name of the law!
Knock, knock
Who's there?
Ewan.
Ewan who?
Nobody else, just me.

Candy Dream

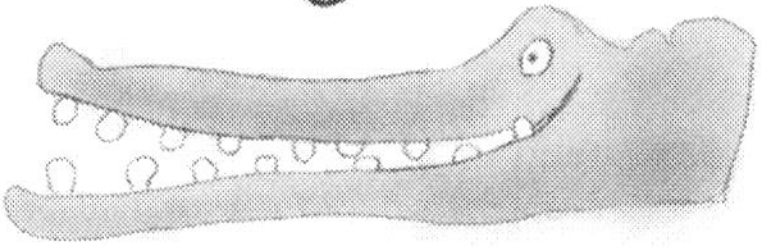

If the world was made of candy
If the world was made of cake
I'd cross the sherbet desert
To reach the chocolate lake
I'd spend the whole day swimming  
With toffee crocodiles
Not one of them is angry
They wear marshmallow smiles
At sunset I'd go skiing
On the Mountain of Sorbet
Then ride a cotton candy cloud
To Treacle Custard Bay
A vanilla fondant pillow
Is wear I'd lay my head
And the sweetest dreams I'd dream
In my cookie crumble bed

Why was the small cookie crying?
Because it's mum had been a wafer so long.
Did you hear about the jelly and sponge who had a punch up?
They were put into custardy.
How did they feel after?
A trifle worried.
Why were the crowd booing at the cookie boxing match?
They were watching crummy fighters!
A triffle worried
Who sits in a bowl and moans about the custard being too hot?
Apple Grumble.
Johnny: what does your dad put on his rhubarb?
Jack: Manure.
Johnny: Yuck, I prefer custard.
Who sits on a cake and sings?
Icing sugar.
aaa

What do you get when two strawberries meet?
A Strawberry shake!

What is white and yellow, and throws itself off the edge of the dinner table?
Lemming Meringue!

Did you hear about the cornflake?
Don't worry I'll tell you next week, it's a cereal.

Boy: Did you like the chocolates Mrs Smith?
Mrs Smith: Yes, very much.
Boy: That's funny. My mum said you didn't have any taste.

What cake wanted to rule the world?
Attila the Bun.

What do you call a rabbit dressed up as a cake?
A cream bun.

How do you grow
a big crop of liquorice?
Plant lots of Ani-seed!
Aniseed
Why was the gingerbread
house in a state of disrepair?
It had been desserted
years ago.
Why was there a lot
of noise in the kitchen?
Because the banana split,
so the ice Screamed!
HELP!
What do you call a
sheep coated in chocolate?
A chocolate baaaa!
How do you lock
the door of a
gingerbread house?
With Coo-keys!
How many idiots does
it take to make chocolate
chip cookies?
Six- One to make the
dough, and five to peel
the M&M's.
How do you start
a Jelly race?
On your marks, Get Set, go!
CHOCOLATE Baa!
MADE IN RAMSGATE

How do elf's make sandwiches?
With shortbread.
Elf
Shortbread
Made with Elf-raising flour
Did you hear about the chocolate factory?
It melted.
What's the best thing to put into a chocolate cake?
Your teeth!
Chocolate
Factory
What candy do fish prefer?
Bubble gum.
What cake gives you an upset stomach?
Rocky road.
How do you make a cream puff?
Chase it around the garden.
How did Hansel and Gretel keep their teeth clean?
With Candy Floss!

Doctor, Doctor

Doctor, doctor
Everyone keeps thinking I'm a liar.
I don't believe you.

Doctor, doctor
I need something to keep my falling hair in.
Here's a bag.

Doctor, doctor
I keep thinking I'm an electric eel.
That's shocking!

Doctor, doctor
I can't get to sleep.
Don't worry, sit on the edge of your bed, you'll soon drop off.

Doctor, doctor
I'm having trouble breathing.
I'll give you something that will soon put a stop to that.

Doctor, doctor
I have amnesia.
Take these pills and you'll soon forget about it.

Doctor, doctor
I keep thinking I'm a needle.
I don't see your point.

Doctor, doctor
I keep thinking I'm a bridge.
What's come over you?
A large truck, two cars and a coach.

Doctor, doctor
What did the X-ray of my head show?
Absolutely nothing.

Mr Krispell's
Favourite Jokes
Fruit
What's purple and
5000 miles long?
The grape wall of China!
What's a librarians
favourite vegetable?
Quite peas.
Time flies like
an arrow.
Fruit flies like
a banana.
How do you
open a
banana?
With a
Monkey!
What did the grape
do when he was stepped on?
He let out a little wine!

Waiter Waiter

Waiter, I think I've just
swallowed a fish bone.
Are you choking?
No, I'm serious.

Waiter, there's a twig
in my meal.
Don't worry, I'll get
the branch manager.

Waiter, why is there
a fish on my plate
of spaghetti?
I'm sorry sir, it
doesn't know it's plaice.

Waiter, what's this?
It's bean soup sir.
I don't care what
it's been, what is it
now?

Waiter, there's a dead fly
swimming in my soup.
Don't be silly, dead
flys can't swim.

Waiter, there's an ant
in my soup.
I know... The flies
stay away during
the winter.

Waiter, this bread
is stale.
It wasn't last week
sir.

Waiter, there's a snail
in my salad.
Don't worry, it won't
eat much.

Doctor, Doctor

Doctor, doctor
My wife smells like a fish.
Poor sole.

Doctor, doctor
I'm a burglar.
Have you taken anything for it?

Doctor, doctor
I've lost my memory.
When did it happen?
When did what happen?

Doctor, doctor
I keep thinking I'm a cowboy.
How long has this been going on?
About a Yeeehaaah!

Doctor, doctor
I feel like a dog.
Sit!

Doctor, doctor
I keep seeing an insect everywhere.
Don't worry—it's just a bug that's going round.

Doctor, doctor
My baby is the image of me.
Not to worry, as long as he's healthy

Doctor, doctor
I keep thinking I'm a caterpillar.
Don't worry, you'll soon change.

Doctor, doctor
I keep seeing double.
Sit on the couch.
Which one?

Doctor, Doctor

Doctor, doctor
I feel like a
pack of cards.
I'll deal with
you later.

Doctor, doctor
I keep thinking
I'm a moth.
So why did you
come here then?
Well, I saw this
Light at the widow.

Doctor, doctor
I get pains in one
eye when I drink
coffee.
Have you tried
taking the spoon out.

Doctor, doctor
People keep on
ignoring me.
Next!

Doctor, doctor
I keep thinking
there are two
of me.
One at a time
please.

Doctor, doctor
Will this ointment
clear up my spots?
I never make
rash promises.

Doctor, doctor
I think I'm a
snail.
Don't worry
we'll soon get you
out of your shell.

Doctor, doctor
My son has just
swallowed a roll
of film.
Let's hope nothing
develops.

Doctor, doctor
I keep thinking
I'm a yo-yo.
Not to worry life's
full of ups and downs.

Weather Fun!

A boy that wasn't that bright
Made his trousers from an old kite
He was ok until
He walked up a hill
Then his trousers blew off and took flight

What do you call
a lovely warm sunny
day following two rainy days?
Monday!
He gets the
weekend off
Why was the
lightning naughty?
He didn't know how
to conduct himself.
Why wouldn't the
cloud talk to the hurricane?
They had a stormy
relationship.
What do you call a
women with a storm
on her head?
Gail.
What animal never
gets wet?
An Umbrellaphant
What's very clever and
fills the sky with Color?
A Brainbow!

Who fell down a rabbit whole and got drenched?
Alice in Thunderland!
What holds the moon up in the sky?
Moonbeams!
What do you call a Snowman on a warm day?
Puddle.
What do you get if you freeze a Witch?
A Cold spell.
Now she's doing Witchdraft
How do sheep keep warm in winter?
They turn on the Central Bleating.
Why shouldn't you ice skate on a full stomach?
Because it's easier to skate on an Ice Rink!
What did one raindrop say to the other?
Two's company, three's a Cloud.

How do you wrap
a cloud?
With a rainbow.
When does it rain
money?
When there's a Change
in the weather.
What do you call
it when it rains,
Chickens and Ducks?
Fowl Weather!
When do monkeys
fall from the sky?
During Ape-ril showers!
What do you call
a Roman Emperor
with a cold?
Julius Sneezer!
What did the tree
say after a long winter?
What a Re-leaf.
Can February March?
No, but April May!

Who invented the first
rain jacket?
Anna Rack!
What's the difference
between a lion with
toothache and a wet day?
One Roars with pain:
the other Pours with rain.
Did you hear about
the idiot who broke his
leg while sweeping leaves?
He fell out of the tree!
↑ Do not use
in trees.
Why don't owls date
when it's raining?
Because it's Too wet too woo!
Where does a Snowman
put his candles?
On his Birthday Flake!
Where did the Snowman
meet his wife?
On the Winternet!
What kind of bow,
can't be untied?
A Rainbow.

Pirate Poetry

Because I wouldn't
marry him
He made me walk
the plank.
I'll love you till
the day you die
He pushed and
then I sank.

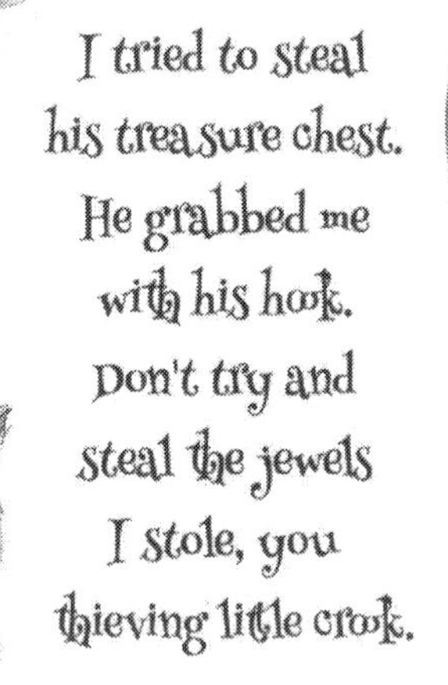

I tried to steal
his treasure chest.
He grabbed me
with his hook.
Don't try and
steal the jewels
I stole, you
thieving little crook.

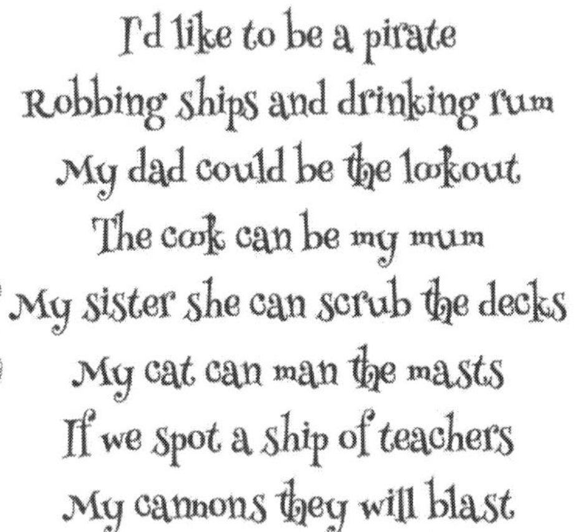

I'd like to be a pirate
Robbing ships and drinking rum
My dad could be the lookout
The cook can be my mum
My sister she can scrub the decks
My cat can man the masts
If we spot a ship of teachers
My cannons they will blast

Why did Captain Hook cross the road?
To get to the second hand shop.
What does a dyslexic pirate say?
Rrrraaaaaa!
How did the pirate get his Jolly Roger so cheaply?
He bought it on sail.
What do you get if you cross Santa Claus with a pirate?
A Yo ho ho.
Why don't pirates shower before they walk the plank?
Because they'll just wash up on the shore later.
What has 7 legs, 7eyes, and 7 arms?
7 pirates.
Why are pirates called pirates?
Because they aaarrrr!

How much did the pirate pay for his peg and hook?
An arm and a leg.

What's orange and sounds like a parrot?
A carrot.

What was the name of Blackbeards wife?
Peg.

Why didn't anybody want to play cards with the pirate?
Because he was standing on the deck.

How do Pirates prefer to communicate?
Aye to aye!

How do you make a pirate furious?
Take away his p. irate.

Have you heard any good pirate jokes?
Well neither have ayyye!

Mr Krispell's Favourite Long Jokes!

Mum: Come on Jack, get dressed; you'll be late for school.
Jack: I don't want to go to school. The teachers don't like me, the children don't like me—even the caretaker doesn't like me!
Mum: You're just being silly.
Jack: Why should I?
Mum: Well, for one thing you're forty three years old, and for another you're the headmaster!

Mum: Why are you crying?
Son: Dad hit his thumb with a hammer.
Mum: Knowing you, I'm surprised you didn't laugh.
Son: That's the problem—I did!

Hee Hee! Ho ho! Hee Hee! Ha ha! Ha ha! Ho ho! Hee Hee! Laughter! Hee Hee! Ho ho! Ha ha! Hee Hee! Ha ha! Ho ho! Hee Hee!

What do you call?
What do you call a man with
a seagull on his head?
Cliff.
What do you call a man with
a rabbit up his jumper?
Warren.
What do you call a girl with
a frog on her head?
Lilly.
What do you call a nun with
a washing machine on her head?
Sister Matic.

Waiter Waiter

Waiter, please be careful your thumb is in my soup.
Not to worry sir, it isn't very hot.

Waiter! What's this footprint doing on my pie?
Waiter: Well you did ask me to step on it, sir.

Waiter, these potatoes taste funny.
Then why aren't you laughing sir?

Waiter, this egg is bad.
Don't blame me sir, I only laid the table.

Waiter! Get me the manager, this food is disgusting.
Waiter: He won't eat it either, sir.

Menu

Waiter, do you serve fish?
Of course sir, we'll serve anyone.

Waiter, bring me something to eat and make it snappy!
Crocodile sandwich on its way, sir.

Waiter, will my pizza be long?
No sir, it'll be round of course.

Waiter Waiter

Waiter, I've just found a
slug in my lettuce!
Don't worry sir we
not charge you extra.

How did you find your
steak, sir?
Well, I just moved a
chip and it was there.

Waiter, what's that fly doing
in my soup?
Appears to be the
backstroke, sir.

Menu

Waiter, do you have
frogs legs?
No it's just the way
I walk.

Waiter, my plates all wet.
That's your soup, madam.

Waiter, what's this fly
doing on my ice cream?
Looks like its learning
to ski sir.

Waiter, is there lasagna
on the menu?
Yes, I'll get a cloth
And wipe it off.

Waiter, there's a wasp
in my soup.
I think you'll find its
a vitamin B.

Waiter Waiter

Waiter, I think I've just swallowed a fish bone.
Are you choking?
No, I'm serious.

Waiter, there's a twig in my meal.
Don't worry, I'll get the branch manager.

Waiter, why is there a fish on my plate of spaghetti?
I'm sorry sir, it doesn't know it's plaice.

Waiter, what's this?
It's bean soup sir.
I don't care what it's been, what is it now?

Waiter, there's a dead fly swimming in my soup.
Don't be silly, dead flys can't swim.

Waiter, there's an ant in my soup.
I know... The flies stay away during the winter.

Waiter, this bread is stale.
It wasn't last week sir.

Waiter, there's a snail in my salad.
Don't worry, it won't eat much.

Crazy Fun!

I once knew a girl called Hannah
Who used to eat food with a spanner
Every time that she ate
She'd smash every plate
In the most peculiar manner

What do you get if you cross a cow with a volcano?
Udder disaster.

Why was the duck sent to the headmasters office?
He kept on making wisequaks.

Why did the nose hate going to school?
Because he was tired of being picked on.

Why wouldn't the bogeyman go out on Friday night?
Because he was all dressed up with nowhere to goo.

He wants to go out and boogie

What do you call a bird that laughs at everyone?
A mockingbird.

Why was the archaeologist crying?
He hit rock bottom because his career was in ruins.

Bang!
Bang!
Bang!
Bang!
Bang!
Who invented a plane
that wouldn't fly?
The Wrong brothers.
Where does Tarzan
get his clothes from?
A jungle sale!
Jungle Sale
Bang!
Bang!
What insects can
tell the time?
Clockroahes!
What do you call a
mad young octopus?
A crazy mixed up squid!
tick tock
How do you cut
an ocean in half?
With a sea-saw.
What's small white
and smells?
A pong pong ball.
Pongy! have you been
playing stable tennis?
Bang!
Bang!
What grows on a wall?
A Walnut!
Bang!
Bang!
Bang!
Bang!
Bang!
Bang

BOMB
Where do butchers dance?
At a meatball.
"We'll meat again"
Why did the stamp need a lawyer?
It was ripped off.
"Don't address me like that!"
Why did the fishmonger go deaf?
He lost his herring.
Why did the elephant leave the circus?
He was tired of working for peanuts.
Did you hear that the fire-eater got engaged?
He ran into an old flame.
"I've got a hot date tonight!"
Where do spies shop?
At the snoopermarket.
Beans
Why did the baker stop making donuts?
He was tired of the hole thing.

Christmas Fun!
Silly sailor Sally
sailed the seven seas
Her sails were sown of silken threads
Her masts of Christmas trees

What did one snowman say to the other.
Do you smell carrots?

What did Adam say the day before Christmas?
It's Christmas Eve.

What's green covered in tinsel and eats flies?
Mistle-toad.

Did you hear about the thief who stole a Christmas calendar?
He got 12 months.

What goes: Now you see me, now you don't, now you see me, now you see me?
A snowman on a Zebra crossing.

How does
Good King Wenceslas
like his pizza?
Deep and crisp and even.

What do you get
if you eat Christmas
decorations?
Tinsell-itis!

The first sign of
Tinselitis

Who did Father
Christmas marry?
Mary Christmas.

Son: Can I have a budgie
for Christmas?
Mum: No, you can have turkey
like the rest of us.

What do guests sing at
a snowman's birthday
party?
Freeze a Jolly Good Fellow.

Why does Father Christmas
come down the chimney?
Because it soots him.

Funny Clothes

I once knew a girl called Eileen
Who lived in a washing machine
She dined with a frock
Then married a sock
And never again was seen

What coat feels wet when you put it on?
A coat of paint!

Gentleman: Can I try those trousers on in the window?
Snooty shop assistant: We'd prefer you tried them on in the changing room, sir!

I stand corrected, said the man in orthopaedic shoes.

Sister: This dress fits me like a bandage.
Brother: Did you buy it by accident?

Where can you buy a cheap elephant?
At a Jumbo sale.

Lady: Do you sell crocodile shoes?
Assistant: what size feet does your crocodile have, madam?

Who's the boss of the hankies?
The Hankie-chief.
What does the Queen do if she burps?
Issues a royal pardon.
Tom: My dad went swimming and all his clothes were stolen.
Jim: So what did he come home in?
Tom: The dark.
Coat of Arms
In which tree should you hang your underwear?
In a pantry– or a vestry!
Why did the opera singer have such a high voice?
She had falsetto teeth.
La La
To whom do people always take off their hats?
Hairdressers.
What coat has many sleeves?
A coat of arms

Sally: Every Time I'm down in the dumps, I get myself a new outfit.
Tom: I was wondering where you got them from.

Did you hear about the two silk worms that had a race?
It ended in a tie!

What do you call a butchers assistant?
A chop assistant.

Sally: For my birthday, I'd like a dress that matches my eyes.
Tom: Where can you buy a bloodshot dress?

Did you hear about the man who put a new pair of shoes on every day?
By the end of the week, he couldn't put his shoes on

What do you get if you pull your underwear up to your neck?
A chest of drawers!

School Fun
I like my teacher very much
She is funny and she's kind
When my dog ate my homework
She didn't seem to mind
The next day with my Homework
She handed me a bone.
And then she gently smiled at me
Clever, funny, Mrs Sloan

Teacher: How did the Vikings communicate with each other?
Pupil: With Norse Code!
Teacher: You have half an hour to write an essay on Hadrian's wall.
Pupil: But miss I'd rather write on paper.
It was built a long time ago!!
Son: Dad, I think my teacher really likes me.
Dad: Whys that son?
She keeps putting kisses on my homework.
Teacher: If I had seven apples in one hand and ten oranges in my other hand what would I have?
Pupil: Very large hands!
Dad: How was your first day at school son.
Son: My new teacher doesn't know anything, all he does is ask questions!
Teacher: What word do you always spell incorrectly?
Pupil: Incorrectly!
School Report

Why did the Elf fail his exams?
He didn't do his Gnome work
Teacher: You, boy, name me two pronouns!
Boy: Who, me?
Teacher: Correct!
Which Queen suffered indigestion?
Queen Hic-toria.
Teacher: Where were traitors beheaded?
Pupil: Just above their shoulders!
Teacher: Does any one know anything about Ancient Greece?
Pupil: They serve it in the canteen miss!
Why did Henry the V111 have so many wife's?
He liked to chop and change.
Ancient grease found in school canteen
Teacher: What does minimum mean?
Pupil: A very small mother!
Minimum
Maximum

Teacher: Paul, did your sister help you with your homework?
Paul: No, miss, she did it all
Teacher: Peter why are you late for school?
Peter: Well Sir, I was walking to school when I saw a sign that said, Slow, school ahead.
SLOW DOWN SCHOOL AHEAD
Warning slow down or you'll end up in class.
Teacher: If I cut a banana into five pieces and a apple into seven pieces what have I got?
Pupil: Fruit salad.
Teacher: Do you know what adding is?
Paul: Yes, miss, that's the noise my door bell makes!
Ding! Ding!
Teacher: Simon can you spell Your name backwards?
Simon: No, miss.
Teacher: This essay on 'My Dog' is exactly the same as your sister's!
Harry: Well it's the same dog.

If there are eight cats in a boat and one jumps out, how many are left?
None, they are all Copycats!
When was Queen Victoria buried?
Just after she died.
What came after the Stone Age?
The Saus-age.
The Saus-age began on a Fryday.
What exam must you pass before you can work in a soda drink factory?
Fizzical education.
Soda
Where are the Kings and Queens of England crowned?
On the head.
Why were the teachers eyes crossed?
She couldn't control her pupils.

Bungee Jumping
By Hugo First

Lumberjacks guide book
By Tim Burr

I Lost My Boot
By Marie Celeste

Fast Food is Good For You!
By Frank Furter

The Invisible Man
By Otto Sight

Best Italian Recipes
By Al Dente

Locksmiths Guide
By Dorris Open

How to get a knighthood
By Neil Down

Coffee is Bad for You!
By T. Pott

Did Pirates Talk Backwards?
By Rodger Jolly

D I Y Bird Table
By Jack Daw

How to have a White Christmas!
By Dan Druff

Catching Crooks
By Hans Upp

Make Your Own Robot
By Anne Droid

Space Poems

A Martian came to Earth
last night
I think I've got the proof
my bedrooms full of greenish slime
and now we've got no roof

I'm going to build a rocket
I'm going to the moon
I've a suitcase full of sandwiches
For I won't be back till June

I'll send school dinners straight to Mars
they'll see what Earthlings eat
we'll see their ships bypass the earth
I guess we'll never meet

What was the first animal in space?
The cow, it jumped over the moon.

Why won't the diners tip at the restaurant on the moon?
It's got no atmosphere.

How does an astronaut say sorry?
He Apollo-gises.

How. Do you have a successful space party?
You planet. (plan it.)

What was the first fruit in space?
A coco-naut

Where can you buy dairy products in space?
The Milky Way.

Where do astronauts kiss at Christmas?
Underneath the missile-toe.

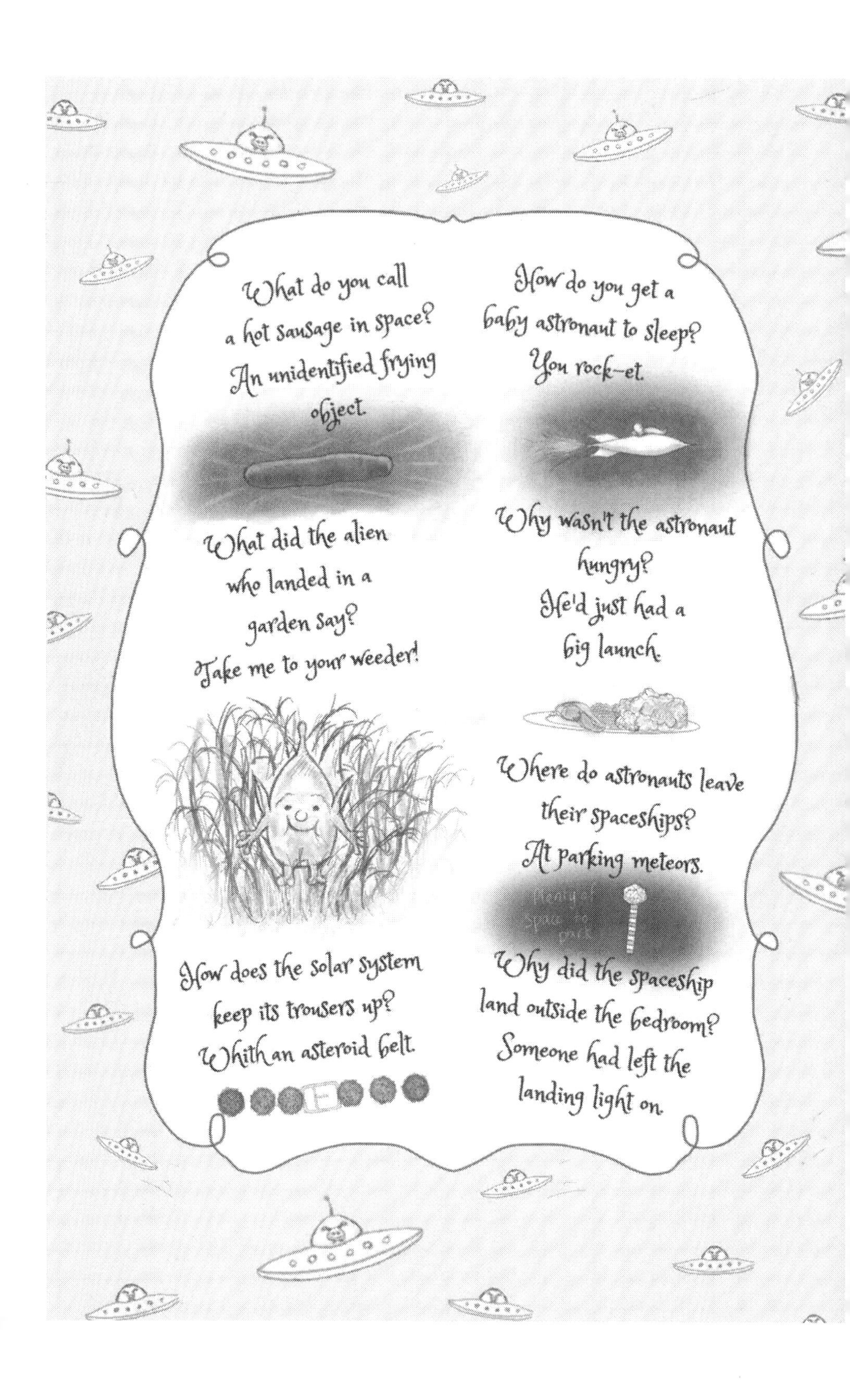
What do you call a hot sausage in space?
An unidentified frying object.
How do you get a baby astronaut to sleep?
You rock-et.
What did the alien who landed in a garden say?
Take me to your weeder!
Why wasn't the astronaut hungry?
He'd just had a big launch.
Where do astronauts leave their spaceships?
At parking meteors.
How does the solar system keep its trousers up?
Whith an asteroid belt.
Why did the spaceship land outside the bedroom?
Someone had left the landing light on.

What do passing shooting stars say to each other?
Pleased to meteor!
Which is heavier: a full moon or half a moon?
A half moon because a full moon is lighter.
What did Mercury say to Saturn?
Give me a ring sometime.
What did Superman's parents ask him when he got home?
Where on earth have you been?
Why are aliens great gardeners?
Because they have green fingers.
Why did the atom cross the road?
Because it was time to split.
When can't you book a room on the moon?
When it's full.

Brother vs Sister

Sister: I always speak my mind.
Brother: I'm surprised you have so much to say then.

Brother: How long can someone live without a brain?
Sister: How old are you?

Brother: Mum, there's a salesman at the door with a funny face.
Sister: Tell him you've already got one!

Sister: None of these matches in this box work!
Brother: That's funny they were all working when I tested them yesterday!

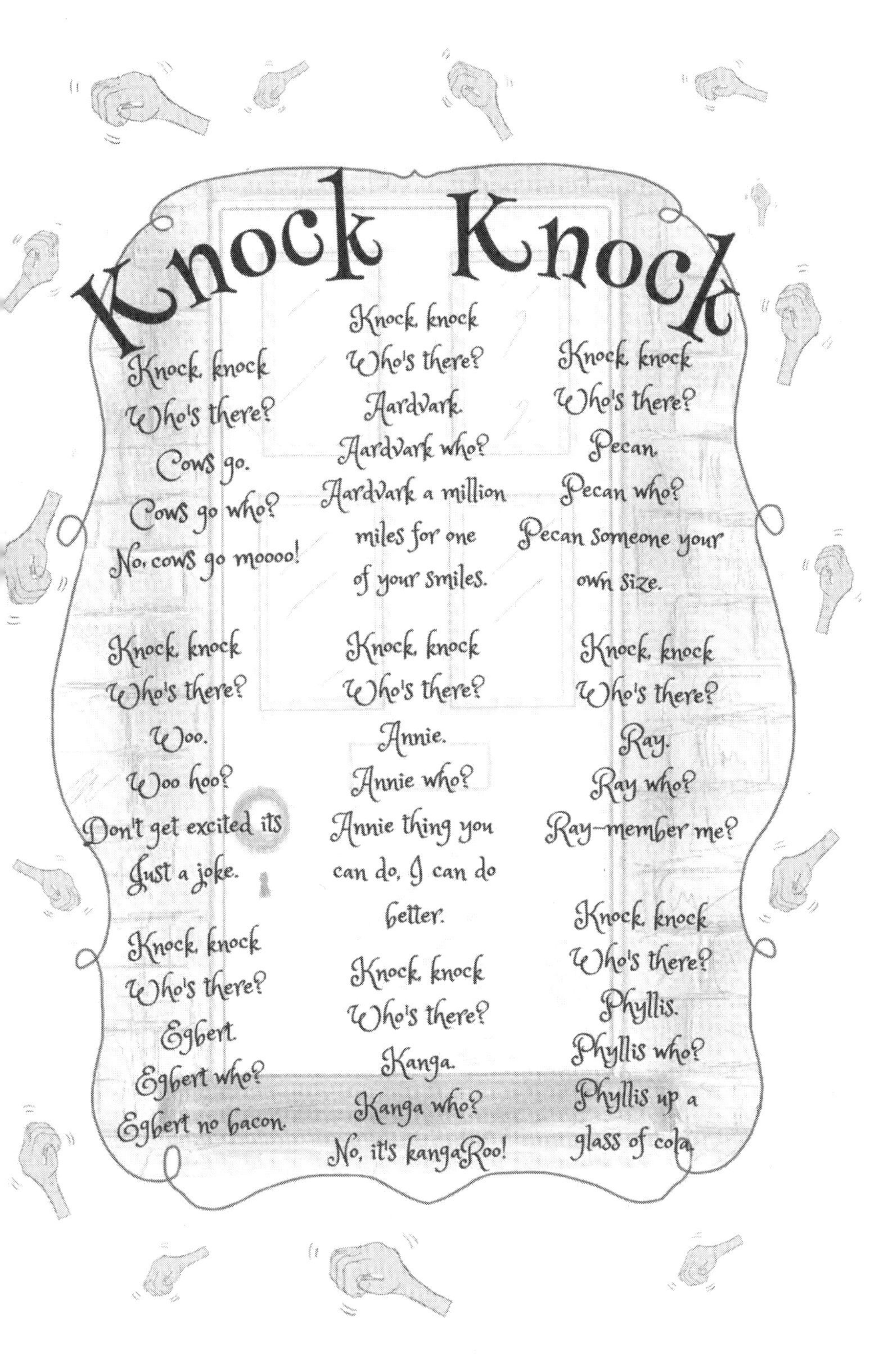
Knock Knock
Knock, knock
Who's there?
Cows go.
Cows go who?
No, cows go moooo!
Knock, knock
Who's there?
Woo.
Woo hoo?
Don't get excited its
Just a joke.
Knock, knock
Who's there?
Egbert.
Egbert who?
Egbert no bacon.
Knock, knock
Who's there?
Aardvark.
Aardvark who?
Aardvark a million
miles for one
of your smiles.
Knock, knock
Who's there?
Annie.
Annie who?
Annie thing you
can do, I can do
better.
Knock, knock
Who's there?
Kanga.
Kanga who?
No, it's kangaRoo!
Knock, knock
Who's there?
Pecan.
Pecan who?
Pecan someone your
own size.
Knock, knock
Who's there?
Ray.
Ray who?
Ray-member me?
Knock, knock
Who's there?
Phyllis.
Phyllis who?
Phyllis up a
glass of cola.

Insect Poetry

Bees give you honey
Bugs give you bites
Worms give you tummy aches
And spiders give you frights

To hide your bugs and insects
You need a secret place
Like your mothers slippers
Or your sisters pillow case

A spider was the head chef
The baker was a snail
They opened up a cake shop
Not one cake did they sell
But our cakes are the finest
They're made with worm and flea
Our loaves are so delicate
Spiced with wasp and bee
Why they never sold one single cake
Remains a mystery

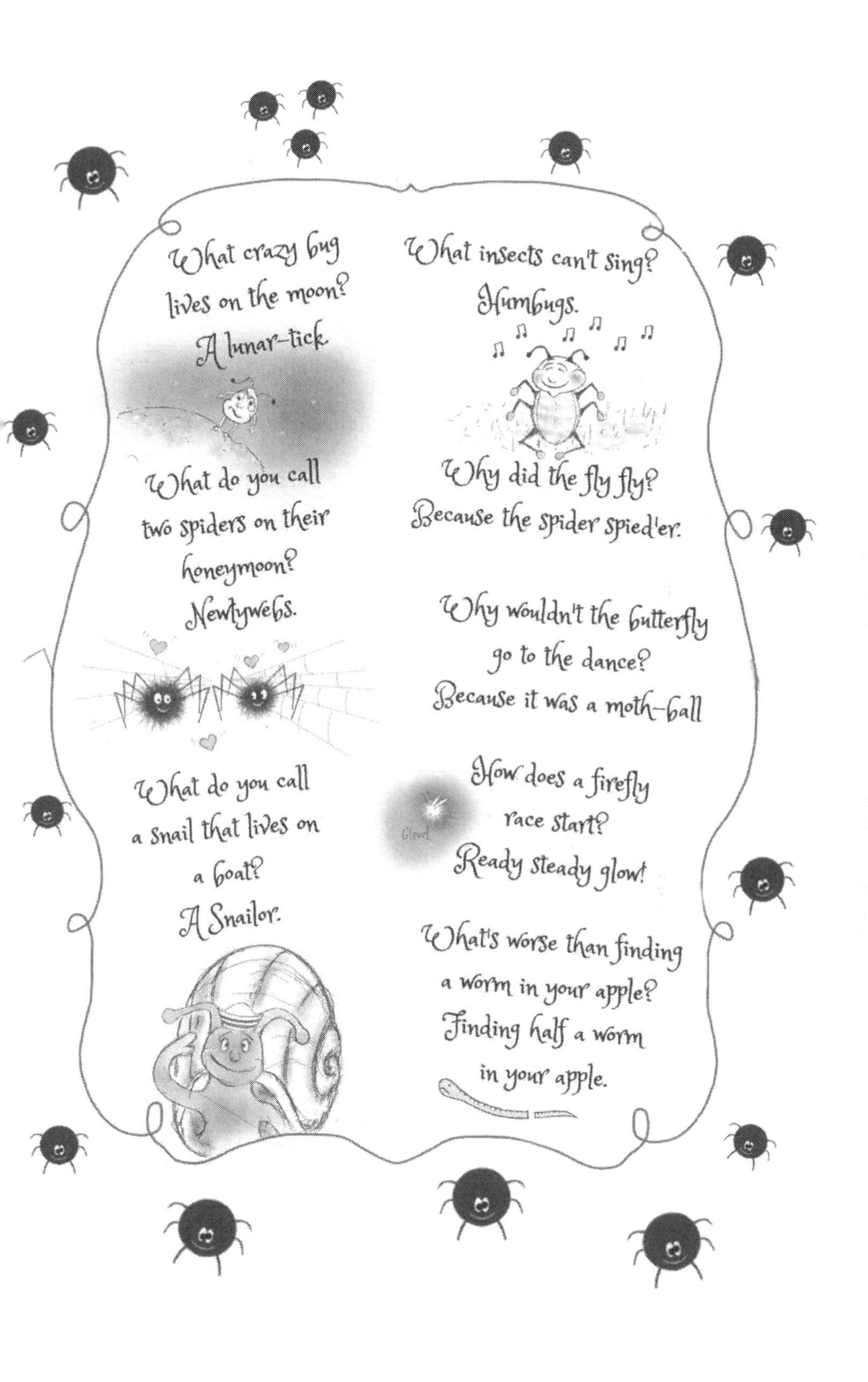
What crazy bug
lives on the moon?
A lunar-tick.
What do you call
two spiders on their
honeymoon?
Newlywebs.
What do you call
a snail that lives on
a boat?
A Snailor.
What insects can't sing?
Humbugs.
Why did the fly fly?
Because the spider spied'er.
Why wouldn't the butterfly
go to the dance?
Because it was a moth-ball
How does a firefly
race start?
Ready steady glow!
What's worse than finding
a worm in your apple?
Finding half a worm
in your apple.

How many legs does an ant have?
Two the same as an uncle.
2 the same as an uncle
What do you get if you cross a parrot with a centipede?
A walkie-talkie.
What are the slowest creatures on Mars?
Snail-ions.
If Martians live on Mars and Venusians live on Venus, what lives on Pluto?
Fleas.
What do you call a greenfly with no legs, arms or wings?
A bogey.
Where would you find Giant snails.
On the need of Giants' fingers!
I couldn't find a frog.
Mum: Bill why did you put a spider in your sister's bed?
Bill: I couldn't find a frog.

What's invisible and jumps up and down in a field all day?
A glass-hopper

You can't see it because it's invisible.

What's the difference between school dinners and worms?
School dinners come on a plate.

What's the last thing That goes through a wasps mind when it hits the windscreen?
It's sting.

"Ouch take him to Waspital."

Why don't baby birds smile?
We'll would you smile if your mum fed you worms all day?

Yuck!

How do you know which end of a worm is its head?
Tickle it and see which end smiles.

How do you keep flies out of the school canteen?
Let them taste the food

This side was tickled.

Slug: Who's that sitting on your back?
Snail: That's Michelle.

Veg Poem

I won't eat turnips
I won't eat peas
I don't like brussels
They make me sneeze
I don't like cabbage or curly Kale
I've heard it makes boys grow a tale
I don't want courgetes
I can't Stand leek
It makes your knees and elbows creak
Carrots onions parsnips foul
They'll turn a smile into a scowl
I don't want spinach or aubergines
I don't want veg or any greens
No broad beans or cauliflower cheese

Triple ice cream and jelly please!

What's slim, green and goes boing-boing-boing?
A spring onion.

Why did the farmer drive a steam roller over his field?
He wanted to grow mashed potatoes.

Why should you never tell a secret in a greengrocer's?
Because the potatoes have eyes and the beanstalk.

Why did the mushroom gat invited to lots of parties?
Because he was a fun guy.

What do hedgehogs have for dinner?
Prickled onions.

What did the courgette who married an onion say?
"I'll love you till the day you fry!"

What purple King ruled over England?
Alfred the Grape!

What did the lemon
say to the orange?
Anything you can do
I can do bitter.
What's yellow and
always points north?
A magnetic banana.
N
E
W
S
How do you make
a peach punch?
Give it boxing lessons.
What fruit teases you
a lot?
A ba..na..na..na..na.
What sits in a fruit
bowl and cries for help?
A damson in distress.
What do you call
an oversized pumpkin?
A plumpkin.
Why was the peanut
crying?
He'd just been asalted.
"That hurt my peelings!"
"Ba-na-na-na-na"

Dinosaur Fun!

At the bottom of my garden
There was a dinosaur asleep
I tickled him under arm
He didn't make a peep
I whistled him ten merry tunes
He didn't even stir
Then I sat a cat upon his ear
He couldn't hear him purr
A mountain of petals
I placed beneath his nose
Pebbles, sticks, and apple cores
I crammed between his toes
Finally from the shed roof
I jumped onto his nose
Then miracle of miracles
The dinosaur arose
He didn't seem that friendly
There was an angry roar
So I refused to play with him
That rude dinosaur!

Where did the T. Rex live?
Anywhere it wanted.
What do you call fossilised bacon?
Jurassic Pork.
How do you cut a Triceratops in half?
With a Dino-saw.
DINO SAW
What bird used to work in a bakery before becoming extinct?
The dough dough bird.
What do you call a dinosaur that eats gunpowder?
A Dino-mite.
Why did the T. Rex wear plasters?
He had Dino-sores.
How do you brush a Sabre toothed tiger's teeth?
Very carefully.

Where can you buy
a T. rex from?
A dino-store.
Dinostore
SALE
What dinosaur was
jailed for rustling cattle?
Tyrannosaurus Tex.
Where would you see
a T-Rex in a Bikini?
At the Dino-shore.
What do you call
a vegetarian dinosaur.
A Brocileasoarus.
How do you know
when there's a Tyrannosaurus
rex in the house?
The Triceratops is missing.
What dinosaur won't
drink coffee?
Tea Rex.
Tea
Rex
cup
What do dinosaurs put
on their fries?
Tomato-saurus.
What do you call
a blind dinosaur?
Doyouthinkhesaurus.

Monster Fun
I dined with a monster I knew
so proud of his big pot of goo
Carrots and bats
Ferrets and rats
I spent the next week on the loo

What's it like to be kissed by a vampire?
A pain in the neck.

What do you do with a green monster?
Wait until he ripens.

Why didn't the two four-eyed monsters marry?
They couldn't see eye to eye.

Why were all the monsters booing in the theatre?
They were watching the Abominable Showman.

Where do you store werewolfs?
In a Were-house.

Why don't monsters eat clowns?
Because they taste funny!

What do you call a nervous witch?
A twitch.

What's a werewolf's favourite day of the week?
Moonday.

Why are graveyards so popular?
Because everybody's dying to get in.

What time does Dracula visit the dentist?
Tooth hurty!

Who did Frankenstein take on a date?
His Goul-friend.

What can you find between Godzilla's toes?
Slow runners!

Why was there no food left at the halloween party?
Because everyone was a goblin

What's the largest building in Transylvania?
The Vampire State Building.

Who do you call
if you've a spooky
bread bin?
Toastbusters!
TOASTBUSTERS
What monster hides
in your handkerchief?
The bogey monster.
Don't worry
he's snot that
Scary!
How do you know
when there's a monster
under your bed?
Your nose touches
the ceiling.
What's the best way
to talk to a monster?
On the phone.
Hi Monster
How ya doing?
1234
5678
90
Why should never upset
a cannibal?
You might get into
hot water.
What do you call a
monster that devours
everything in his path?
Lonely.

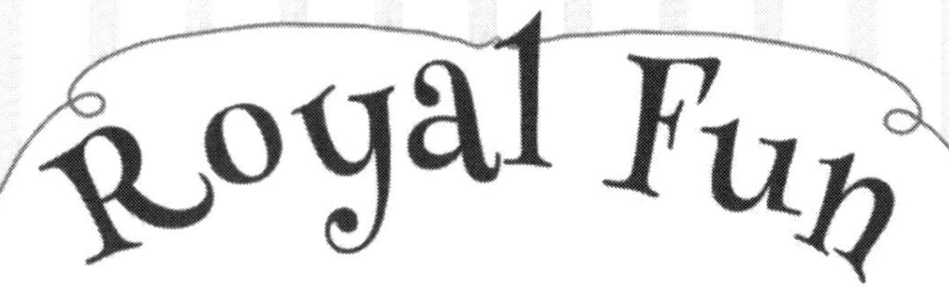

Royal Fun

I once knew a Queen who was barmy
She wore a dress of salami
But by the end of the week
The whole palace did reek
And she was marched to the bath
By her army

Pupil: I wished I'd lived in the olden days.
Teacher: Why?
Pupil: There wouldn't be so much history to learn.

When was King Arthur's army too tired?
When they'd had too many sleepless Knights.

Which Queen of England had the largest crown?
The one with the largest head.

What's the difference between the death rates of the Middle Ages and today?
There isn't, it's still one death per person.

What did one knife say to the other?
Look sharp.

Why are soldiers so tired on April 1st?
They've just completed a 31 day March.

What did the executioner say to his wife?
Only 30 chopping days before Christmas.
What does the Queen do after she burps?
Issues a royal pardon.
Why did the Queen go to the dentist?
To get her teeth crowned.
Where did King Charles keep his armies?
Up his sleevies.
Who invented King Arthur's round table?
Sir Cumference.
Inventor →
Why did the Queen draw straight lines?
Because she's a ruler.
A STRAIGHT TALKING QUEEN
During which battle was Lord Nelson killed?
His last one.
Who invented fractions?
Henry the Eighth.

Mr Krispell's Favourite Long Jokes!

Hairdresser: How would you like it, Madam?
Lady: Could you cut it very short on one side and not at all on the other, with a short stubby fringe at the front and big tufts pulled out at the back?
Hairdresser: Oh dear, I don't think I can manage that, madam.
Lady: Why not? You did last time.

One day, two big tortoises and a little tortoise went into a café. They ordered three strawberry milkshakes. While they were waiting it began to rain.
'Oh dear,' said one of the big tortoises. 'We should have brought our umbrella.' 'Yes' said the other big tortoise. 'Let's send the little one back to get it.'
'I'll go,' said the little tortoise, 'but promise me you won't drink my strawberry milkshake while I'm away.'
Well the two big tortoises promised not to touch his strawberry milkshake, and the little tortoise set off.
A few days later one the big tortoises said 'let's eat his strawberry milkshake anyway.' At that moment the little tortoise shouted from the back of the café, 'You do that and I won't fetch the umbrella!'

Ho ho! Hee Hee! Ha ha! Laughter!

Music Fun
Why was the musician arrested?
He got into treble.
Why are pianos grand?
Because they're so upright!
Did you hear about the boy who played recorder in tune?
Neither did I.
What's a cats favourite musical?
The sound of mew-sic.
Piano tuner: I've come to tune your piano.
Pianist: But I didn't call you.
Piano tuner: No but your neighbours did.
What do you call a piano with only white keys?
A minor problem!
What vegetable has great rhythm?
Beat-root.

I joined the sea scouts of Kent
But we camped under sea in a tent
"It's no use complaining,
at least it's not raining"
Said the scout leader of Kent

What kind of hair does the ocean have?
Wavy.

What's got one large hand, one small hand and sharp teeth?
A Clock-adile!

Why do fish like worms?
Because they're hooked on them!

What day do fish hate most?
Fryday!

What did the fish call his date?
His Gill-friend.

What did the boat call her date?
Her buoy-friend.

Who stole the baby octopus?
A Squidnapper.

What lies at the bottom of the sea shivering?
A nervous wreck.

What do you call a frog with no hind legs?
Un-hoppy.

Where does a sick ship go?
To the dock.

ALL SEA SICK SHIPS REPORT TO DOCK!

What kind of cats love water?
Octopuses!

Doctor, doctor I smell like a fish!
Oh you poor sole!

Where would you weigh a whale?
At a Whale Weigh Station!

Did you hear about the cargo ship carrying potatoes, that run aground in a storm?
It caused a giant Chip wreck!

What do you call
a man with a seagull
on his head?
Cliff!
What do you call
a girl with a bucket
and spade on her head?
Sandy!
What do you call a
man floating in the sea?
Bob!
Why was the
mermaid so bitter?
She grew up with
a ship on her shoulder!
What did the small sardine
say when it saw a submarine?
Look mum a tin of people!
Tinned People
Yummy!
Why did the bird
sit on the fish?
The fish was Perch!
Why does it take pirates
so long to learn the Alphabet?
They spend years at C.

Why does the ocean Roar?
Well, wouldn't you if you had crabs on your bottom!
Mum; How are your marks at school Bill?
Bill; They're underwater.
Mum; What?
Bill; They're below C.
How far can a pirate ship go?
20 miles to the Galleon.
2 4 8 5
Pirate Petrol
Why was the lobster sent to jail?
He kept on Pinching things!
How much do Pirates pay for their earrings?
A Buccaneer!
€1 →
What do you get if you cross a river with a sea?
Wet!
Who's in jail at the bottom of the sea?
Billy the Squid!
What was his crime?
He robbed a river bank!
WANTED
Billy the Squid
for 8 armed robbery

Looney Fun
Snotty nosed Sarah
Sneezed a snotty sneeze
She sneezed bogeys on the flowers
She sneezed bogeys on the trees
If you want to find her garden
It's easy to be seen
For in every single season
Her garden is still Green

What do you call
a sheep that's going mad?
Baaa-rmy!

Two ducks are on a motorbike.
The one on the back says, 'Quack'
and the other one says, I'm
going as quack as I can.

Dinner:My fish isn't cooked.
Waiter: How do you know?
Dinner: It's eaten all my chips

Who's safe when a
man eating tiger is
on the loose?
Women and children.

What did the policeman
eat for lunch?
Truncheon meat.

Did you hear about
the man who drowned in
a bowl of muesli?
He was pulled under
by a strong currant!

What goes to bed
with its shoes on?
A horse.
Which is the laziest
mountain in the world?
Everest.
What do you call
a failed lion tamer?
Claude Bottom.
A man goes into a
pet shop and says, 'I'd
like to buy a wasp please'.
'Sorry sir. We don't sell
wasps.' 'Well you've got one
in the window.'
Taxi driver: Please can
you tell me if my indicators
are working?
Passenger: Yes, no, yes, no, yes
no, yes, no,
What are brown and
sneak around the kitchen?
Minced spies!

What happens if you fall asleep under a car?
You wake up oily in the morning!
Why did the germ cross the microscope?
To get to the other slide.
What lives in a pod and is a Kung-fu expert?
Bruce Pea.
What do you do when the forth bridge collapses?
Build a fifth bridge.
5
5
These photographs you've taken don't do me justice.
You don't want justice you want mercy.
What do you call a blind reindeer?
No eye deer.

If Kittens
were mittens
They'd make the
the purr-fect gift

If lions
were irons
All creases soon
would shift

If Tigers
were taxis
You wouldn't want
a lift

What do you call
a women with a cat
on her head?
Kitty.
What do you get if
you cross a cat with
a lemon?
A sourpuss.
A very bitter
cat
What's a cats favourite
TV programme?
Mews at ten.
1st cat: What have you done
for your fleas?
2nd cat: Nothing, why should
I? They've never done
anything for me.
Jim: I'm looking for
a one eyed cat called
Tibbles.
Jack: What's the other
eye called?
Jim: What's the difference between
A cats litter tray and a pizza?
Jack: I don't know.
Jim: I'm not coming to dinner
at your house then!

Bill: We had to have our cat put down.
Jack: Was she mad?
Bill: Well, she wasn't too pleased.

Why shouldn't you stand on a cat's tail?
It hurts it's felines.

Bill: Our cat's just like one of the family.
Jack: Really? Which one?

What cat should you never play cards with?
A cheetah.

Jack: Have you ever seen a fox trot?
Bill: No, but I've seen a cat nap.

Mum: Did you put the cat out?
Bill: Was it on fire again?

Bill: In the park I was surrounded by lions.
Jack: Lions in the park?
Bill: Yes, dandelions

Elephant Fun!

Excuse me Mr Elephant
I wonder if you know
You're feet are rather heavy
And ones upon my toe.
I'm from a land called England
We don't like to make a scene
But if you do not move it
I will have to **SCREAMMM!**

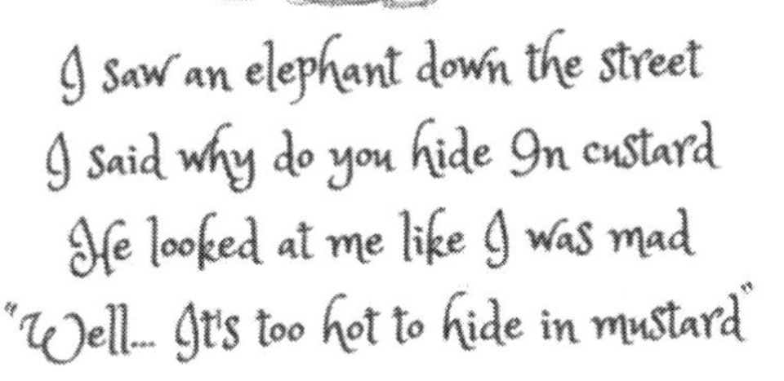

I saw an elephant down the street
I said why do you hide In custard
He looked at me like I was mad
"Well... It's too hot to hide in mustard"

Why is an elephant so wrinkled?
Have you ever tried to fit one on an ironing board?

What do an elephant and a strawberry have in common?
They're both red except for the elephant.

What happened after Ray was stepped on by an elephant?
He became an X-ray.

Why didn't the elephant enjoy his holiday?
The airline lost his trunk.

How do you get down from an elephant?
You don't, you get down from a duck.

Why did the elephant paint his feet yellow?
So he could hide upside down in custard.

Did you hear about the elephant that had a nervous breakdown? They had to give him trunquilizers!
Trunquilizers
What do you call an elephant in a phone booth? Stuck.
What's large, gray and hard to spot? A stain resistant elephant.
What goes up slowly and down quickly? An Elephant in an elevator.
What did the elephant say when he walked into the grocery store? Ouch!
Grocery Store
Waiter! What's this elephant doing in my alphabet soup? Waiter: I guess he's learning to read.
Elementary English

Love Fun!

I once knew a Prince too small
Who loved a Princess too tall
He grew sadder and sadder
Until he found a ladder
And took it along to the ball

What do you sing when two cookies get married?
Here crumbs the bride.

Boy: I told my girlfriend that she was drawing her eyebrows to high.
Friend: Then what happened?
She looked surprised.

Girlfriend:
Whisper something soft and sweet in my ear.
Boyfriend:
Lemon meringue pie.

Boy: Do you have a date for Valentine's Day.
Girl: Yes, February 14th.

What did one boat say to the other?
Are you up for a little row-mance.

Knock, knock
Who's there?
Olive.
Olive who?
Olive you and I don't care who knows it.

Did you hear about the two turnips that got engaged?
They became Swedehearts.

Train Announcement
The train now arriving on platforms
3, 4, and 5 is coming in Sideways!
COMING IN
SIDEWAYS!
TRAIN
INFORMATION
How can you tell
If a train has just
passed you?
You can see it's tracks.
Why are railroad
tracks angry?
Because people are
always crossing them.
Chew
Chew
What do you call
a train that eats toffee?
A chew, chew train.
Miss Stuffy: Porter, how long will
the next train to Inverness be?
Porter: About 150 metres madam.
150 metres

What do you give a
sick lemon?
Lemonade.

Who's at the door?
A man with a drum kit.
Tell him to beat it.

What did the first
mind reader say to
the second mind reader?
You're alright how am I?

I've lost my memory.
When did you lose it?
When did I lose what?

What do you give a
sick bird?
Tweetment.

If two's company and
three's a crowd, what's
four and five?
Nine.

How did the Cowboy
count his livestock?
With a Cow-culator.
2+8
C-O-W
What do Cowboys
put on their salad?
Ranch Dressing
Ranch Dressing
Why did the Indian
ride his horse?
It was to heavy to
carry.
Did you hear about
the two cowboy bakers?
They had a Bun fight
at the O.k. Corral.
How!
I can make you speak
like a red indian.
How?
See I told you I could.
Why did the Cowboys
car break down?
It had Injun trouble.
(engine trouble)

Who made the
Co Co pop?
The cereal killer.
Bad
Cornflake
Why can't Bruce
Wayne get a date?
Because he has Bat Breath.
YUCK!
Where did Superman
meet his girlfriend?
Down Lois Lane.
Lois Lane
What was the Ninja
doing at the doctors?
He had Kung-flu.
Where did Spider-Man
meet his girlfriend? On
the World Wide Web.
WWW Dating
Who fights villains in
a stained shirt?
Souperman.
He will
Ketchup with
criminals eventually
Souper
Man
Why did Tommy throw
his clock out of the window?
He wanted to see time fly.

Where do you send
an injured bee?
To a Waspital.
What does a snail
do on his birthday?
He Shellebrates!
"Happy Birthday
to you, your brain's
full of goo!"
How do you find where
a flea has bitten you?
Start from scratch.
What do bees chew?
Bumble Gum.
Bumble Gum
How do bees get
to school?
On the school buzz.
How does a Nit get
from place to,place?
By Itch-hiking!
Where did Noah keep
his bees on his Ark?
In the Arc-hives.

Strange Library
Win Gold in Relay!
By Anne Dover Baton
Someone Stole my Guitar
By A.K. Pella
Mountains are Dangerous!
By Cliff Hanger
Libary Etiquette
By Danielle Soloud
How to be a Mummy's Boy
By Molly Coddled
I Went Bankrupt
By Owen Cash
I Got Stung
By B. Keeper

Carpet fitting
By Walter Wall

Solving Toothaches
By Phil McCavity

Amazing Breakfast
In Ten Minutes
By Hammond Deggs

The Art of Deception
By Miss Leed

The Perfect Coffee
By Phil Turr

FIGHT BACK AGAINST COLDS!
BY RON E NOSE

Write a Bestseller!
By Paige Turner

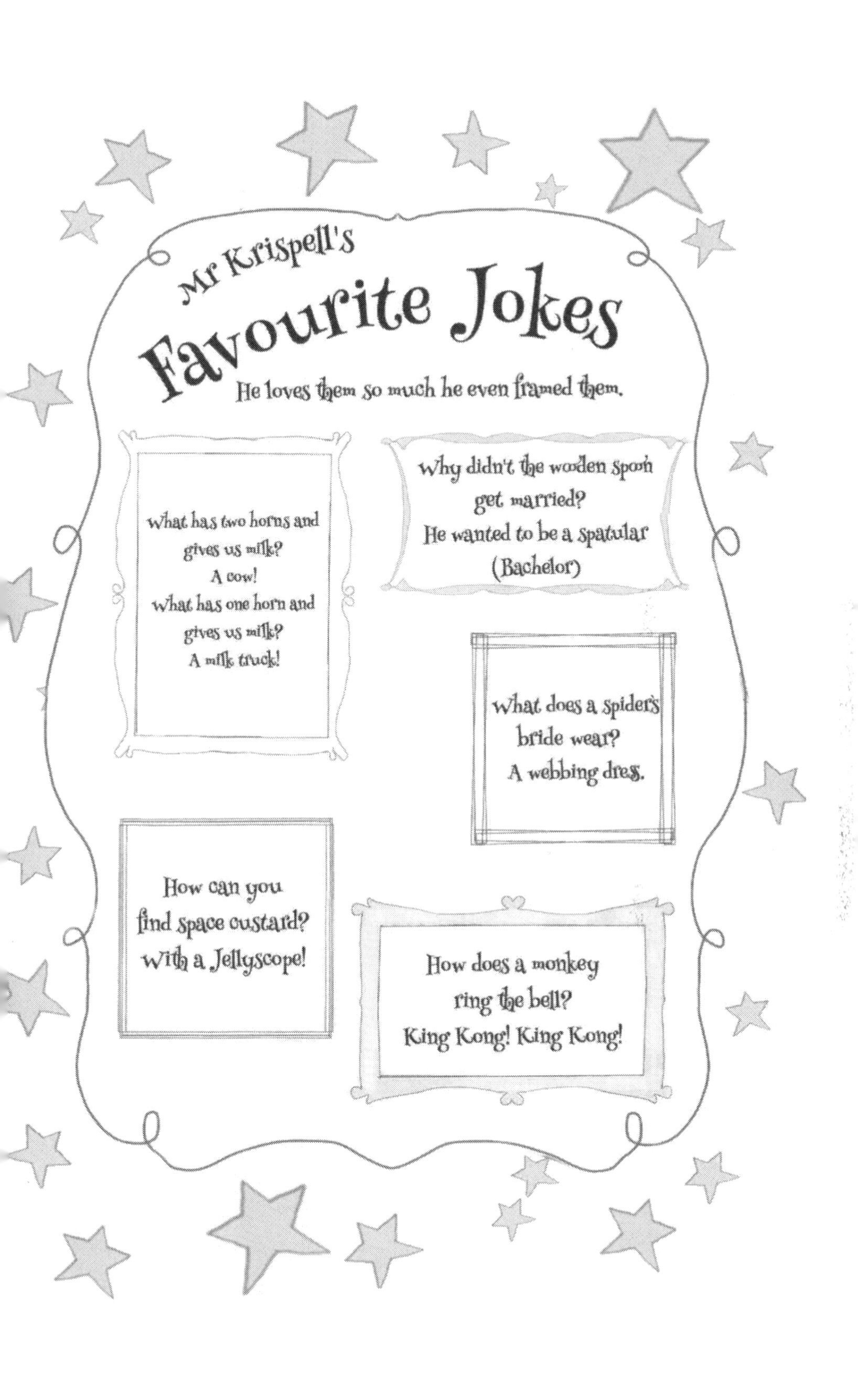
Mr Krispell's
Favourite Jokes
He loves them so much he even framed them.
What has two horns and gives us milk?
A cow!
what has one horn and gives us milk?
A milk truck!
Why didn't the wooden spoon get married?
He wanted to be a spatular (Bachelor)
What does a spider's bride wear?
A webbing dress.
How can you find space custard?
With a Jellyscope!
How does a monkey ring the bell?
King Kong! King Kong!

Mr Krispell's
Favourite Jokes
He loves them so much he even framed them.
What's green misty
and croaks?
Kernite the fog!
What's pink and
cloudy?
A pink cloud.
What's blue and
cloudy?
A pink cloud
holding its breath!
What's E.T
short for?
He has
little legs!
What's blue and
smells like
red paint?
Blue paint.
What should people
who live in glass houses do?
Put the toilet in
the cellar.

What do you call?

What do you call a man with
a number plate on his head?

Reg.

What do you call a woman with
two toilets on her head?

Lulu.

What do you call a Queen with
a heavy lopsided crown on her head?

Queen Eileen.

What do you call a camel with
no hump?

Humphrey!

What do you call?

What do you call a man with potatoes, meat and gravy on his head?

Stew.

What do you call a man with no legs?

Neil.

What do you call a man with leaves on his head?

Russell.

What do you call a man with a bag of compost on his head?

Pete.

What do you call a man with a car on his head?

Jack.

I love my uncle even though He's very Silly!

One day he took up tap dancing.
But he fell into the sink!

He bought a lovely tie from a shop.
But took it back because it was too tight.

He bought a pair of water skis.
Then got fed up when he couldn't find a lake with a slope.

He got sacked from his job at the banana factory.
He kept on throwing all the bent bananas out!

He bought a two piece jigsaw puzzle.
He never finished it because he lost the lid!

He failed at climbing Mount Everest.
He said he ran out of scaffolding!

One day he fell out of a window and broke his leg.
He was ironing the curtains!

MY UNCLE

Tongue Twisters

They are harder than they look!
Try and do these in ten minutes.
Why not get someone to time you...

Toasted treacle tigers taste terrific

Frozen fleas weren't free to flee

Tenderly tickled teapots, tend to tumble out tea hee

Peculiar Petula from Peru parcelled pickled parrots to Timbuktu

Two witches, two watches, which witch wore what watch ?

General Gerald generally generalised in January

Greedy grinning goblins grab ginormous grubs

Terribly tough tongue twisters tend to give tired tongues blisters!

Congratulations!

Very Silly Signs!

All these signs are real!

Outside a chip shop:

WE FOUND NEMO.
FISH SANDWICHES
ARE BACK!

Sign in men's toilet:

WE AIM TO KEEP THESE
TOILETS CLEAN!
YOUR AIM WILL HELP!

Sign inside a shop:

ANYONE
CAUGHT EXITING
THRU THIS DOOR
WILL BE ASKED
TO LEAVE!

Sign outside a house:

BEWARE OF
THE DOG!
THE CAT IS NOT
TRUSTWORTHY
EITHER.

Sign in delicatessen:

Our tongue
sandwiches speak
for themselves!

Outside safari:

BEWARE

WILD
ANIMALS/
CHILDREN

Very Silly Signs!

All these signs are real!

Sign outside office:

ATTENTION

THE FIFTH FLOOR HAS TEMPORARILY BEEN MOVED TO THE SEVENTH FLOOR!

Sign outside shop:

Come in We're **CLOSED**

Sign inside a park:

No signs Allowed!

Sign outside a hotel:

FREE WI-FI

STARTING AT €59 DOLLARS

Sign down a street:

KEEP

RIGHT

Sign outside flats:

Warning!

Bicycles chained to these railings will be moved without notice

THIS IS A NOTICE!

The Jokes I left out!

I didn't tell you the joke about the bed.
Because it hasn't been made yet!

I didn't mention the joke about the dustbin.
Because it's rubbish!

I left out the joke about Pinocchio's nose
Because it was too long!

I left out the joke about the blunt pencil.
Well there's no point!

I was going to tell you the joke about the old mans foot.
But it's too corny.

I decided not to mention the joke about the drill!
It's too boring!

And the funny joke about butter?
I thought you'll only spread it.

A ship carrying red paint collided today with a ship carrying brown paint. Both crews were marooned.
A robber stole a van load of soap today. Police say they tried their best to capture him but he made a clean getaway.

Today we talk to an out of work contortionist who says he can no longer make ends meet.

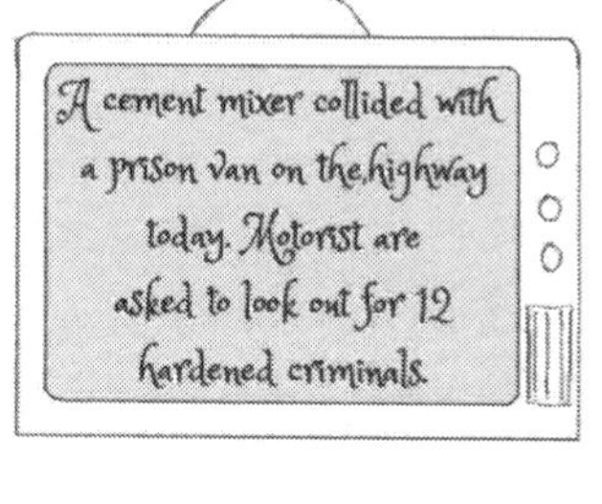

A cement mixer collided with a prison van on the highway today. Motorist are asked to look out for 12 hardened criminals.

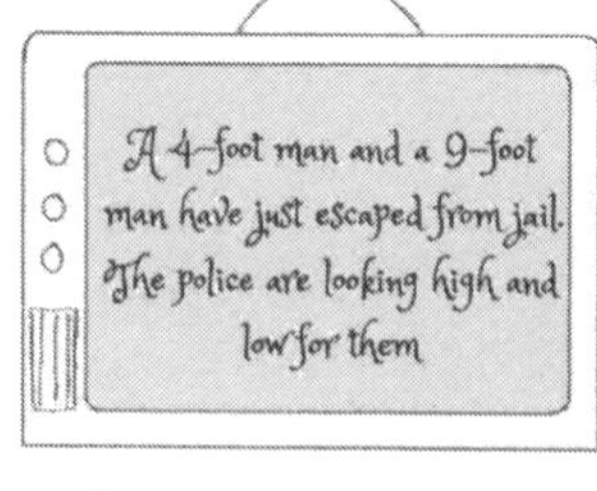

A 4-foot man and a 9-foot man have just escaped from jail. The police are looking high and low for them

A Lorry load of wigs have been stolen in New York. Police are combing the area.

I hope enjoyed reading this book
as much as I did writing it!

Thanks to Charlotte C for additional
poetry stardust.

Mr Krispell is also author of:

Grumble Mumble Grumble

The Princess Everything Book

Why won't Arnold come out to play?

If you're loosing sheep go find a shepherd
If you're loosing sleep go find a good shepherd!

Mr. Krispell Books
Maida Vale, London
rakispell@gmail.com

Editor & additional poetry stardust: **Charli Wood**

Mentor & page layout: **bndn**

Printed in Great Britain
by Amazon